W9-CFB-658

3 1668 03432 8168

CEN   PICTURE BOOKS WELLS
   2008
Wells, Rosemary
Voyage to the Bunny Planet

Central   02/28/2008

CENTRAL LIBRARY

Voyage to the Bunny Planet

Voyage
to the
Bunny Planet

ROSEMARY WELLS

Viking

VIKING

Published by Penguin Group

Penguin Young Readers Group, 345 Hudson Street, New York, New York 10014, U.S.A.

Penguin Group (Canada), 90 Eglinton Avenue East, Suite 700, Toronto, Ontario, Canada M4P 2Y3

(a division of Pearson Penguin Canada Inc.)

Penguin Books Ltd, Registered Offices: 80 Strand, London WC2R 0RL, England

First Tomato, Moss Pillows, and *The Island Light* first published as separate volumes in 1992
by Dial Books for Young Readers, a division of Penguin Books USA
This single-volume edition, with additional material, first published in 2008 by Viking,
a division of Penguin Young Readers Group

1   3   5   7   9   10   8   6   4   2

Copyright © Rosemary Wells, 1992, 2008
All rights reserved

LIBRARY OF CONGRESS CATALOGING-IN-PUBLICATION DATA
Wells, Rosemary.
Voyage to the Bunny Planet / by Rosemary Wells.
p. cm.
Previously published in 3 vols. in 1992, under titles: The island light;
First tomato; and Moss pillows. With new text added.
Summary: Sad bunny children are cheered up when they are transported by the
benevolent Bunny Queen to the magical Bunny Planet,
where they experience their bad days as they should have been.
ISBN 978-0-670-01103-2 (hardcover)
[1. Rabbits—Fiction.] I. Title. PZ7.W46843Vo 2008
[E]—dc22   2007024781

Manufactured in China
Set in Caslon 224
Hand lettering of the title and author's name by Judythe Sieck

JANET BECOMES
THE BUNNY QUEEN

Far beyond the moon and stars
Twenty light-years south of Mars
Spins the gentle Bunny Planet
And the Bunny Queen is Janet.

Born with an amazing ear
She heard what no one else could hear—
Children who had lost their way

Always she was heard to say . . .

"Here's the place where we begin,
On the day that should have been."
Floating in her starry dome,
Janet comes to take us home.

FIRST TOMATO

THE BUNNY PLANET IN HISTORY

*It is the first duty of a flagging spirit to seek renewal
in the latitudes of whimsy. I, for one, dream on
beyond the five planets to a world without wickedness;
verdant, mild, and populated by amiable lapins.*

Benjamin Franklin (Letters to a nephew, 1771)

Claire ate only three spoons
of cornflakes for breakfast.

On the way to school
her shoes filled with snow.

By eleven in the morning,
math had been going on for two hours.

Lunch was Claire's least favorite—
baloney sandwiches.

At playtime Claire was the only girl
not able to do a cartwheel.
Once again the bus was late.

Claire needs a visit to the Bunny Planet.

Far beyond the moon and stars,
Twenty light-years south of Mars,

Spins the gentle Bunny Planet
And the Bunny Queen is Janet.

19

Janet says to Claire, "Come in.

Here's the day that should have been."

I hear my mother calling when the summer wind blows,
"Go out in the garden in your old, old clothes.

Pick me some runner beans and sugar snap peas.
Find a ripe tomato and bring it to me, please."

A ruby red tomato is hanging on the vine.

If my mother didn't want it, the tomato would be mine.

It smells of rain and steamy earth and hot June sun.
In the whole tomato garden it's the only ripe one.
I close my eyes and breathe in its fat, red smell.

I wish that I could eat it now and never, never tell.
But I save it for my mother without another look.

I wash the beans and shell the peas

and watch my mother cook.

I hear my mother calling when the summer winds blow,

"I've made you First Tomato soup because I love you so."

Claire's big warm bus comes at last.
Out her window Claire sees the Bunny Planet
near the evening star in the snowy sky.
"It was there all along!" says Claire.

MOSS PILLOWS

THE BUNNY PLANET IN HISTORY

The captain fell at daybreak, and 'e's ravin' in 'is bed,
With a regiment of rabbits on the planets round 'is 'ead.

Rudyard Kipling (Requiem, 1892)

Robert had to ride in the backseat of the car for four hours of turnpike driving.

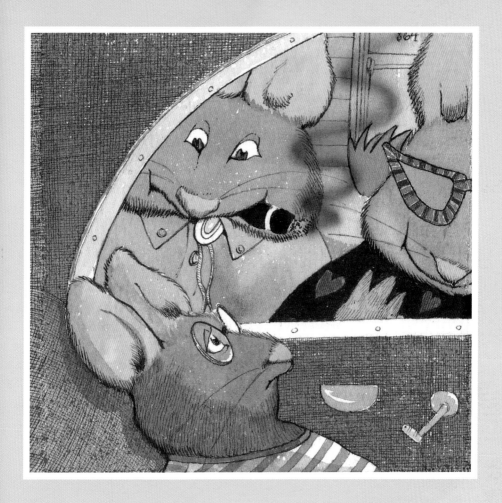

He and his family arrived at Uncle Ed and Aunt Margo's at 3:30 in the afternoon on the first Sunday in February.

Ed and Margo's four boys all piled on top of him at once.

Just before dinner Ed and Margo
were bitten by the argument bug.

Dinner was cold liver chili.
All evening Robert had to hide from the boys.

Robert needs a visit to the Bunny Planet.

Far beyond the moon and stars,
Twenty light-years south of Mars,

Spins the gentle Bunny Planet
And the Bunny Queen is Janet.

"Robert," Janet says. "Come in.

THE BUNNY PLANET

PILLOWS

MOSS

Here's the day that should have been."

All of a sudden I disappear

To my house in a sweet-gum tree.
Where I sing to myself in the whispering woods,
And nobody's there but me.

I sing, "O what a beautiful morning!"
to a chorus of beetles and birds.

Then I play my woodwhistle clarinet
in the parts where I don't know the words.

The kitchen is my favorite room.
It's easy to keep it clean.
I have a secret recipe for toasted tangerine.

Place the sections on a log, directly in the sun.
Wait until they're warm and crisp.
Eat them when they're done.

Deep in a pocket of emerald moss
I lie where the leaves fall free.

My pillow is soft as milkweed
And as green as a tropical sea.

I read the colors in the leaves,
The clouds that roam the sky.

I read the footprints in the sand
To see who's wandered by.

Robert rides home very late.
He sees the Bunny Planet through the car window,
behind the moon in the winter sky.
"It was there all along!" says Robert.

THE
ISLAND LIGHT

THE BUNNY PLANET IN HISTORY

I designated this heavenly body "Coniglio,"
but alas, never saw it again.

Galileo (Diary entry, January 1, 1599)

Felix was sick in front of the whole art class.

The nurse made him a cup of tea and called home.
Nobody answered the phone.
Felix burned his tongue on the tea.

That afternoon the doctor gave Felix medicine
that tasted like gasoline.
Felix's mother and the nurse had to hold him
down for a shot.

Later Felix was accidentally soaked by an icy shower.

Felix's father was busy in the cellar with the boiler.
Felix's mother was busy finding a plumber.
Both forgot to kiss him good night.

Felix needs a visit to the Bunny Planet.

Far beyond the moon and stars,
Twenty light-years south of Mars,

Spins the gentle Bunny Planet
And the Bunny Queen is Janet.

"Felix," Janet says. "Come in.

Here's the day that should have been."

The mailboat comes at six o'clock.
I walk my father to the dock.

The boat brings apples, milk, and flour,
And sails back home within an hour.

A squall is stirring up the sky.
Our lighthouse home is warm and dry.

The light was built in nineteen-ten.
It's had six keepers here since then.

We're wet and salty, but who cares?
Our sweaters dry on kitchen chairs.

We mix an apple pancake batter,
Singing while the shutters clatter.

The night wind howls. The rain leaks in.
After supper we play gin.

Our sweaters steam. The fire crackles.
The ocean swells and lifts its hackles.

We split a piece of gingerbread
And play another round in bed.

Outside the sea enfolds the sand.
Inside I hold my father's hand.

Felix wakes at midnight.
Out his bedroom window he sees the Bunny Planet
near the Milky Way in the summer sky.
"It was there all along!" says Felix.